CW00924788

THE BLACK-SAND MINERS

By the same author

(Gazelles)
Dragon Fire
Dragon Water
Dragon Air
Dragon Earth

(Antelopes)
The Horse Tree

THE BLACK-SAND MINERS

by

ANN RUFFELL

Illustrated by Trevor Stubley

HAMISH HAMILTON
LONDON

For Selina

First published in Great Britain 1985 by
Hamish Hamilton Children's Books
Garden House 57–59 Long Acre London WC2E 9JZ
Copyright © 1985 by Ann Ruffell
Illustrations © 1985 by Trevor Stubley

British Library Cataloguing in Publication Data
Ruffell, Ann
The black-sand miners.—(Antelope series)
I. Title II. Stubley, Trevor
823'.914[J] PZ7
ISBN 0–241–11502–7

Filmset in Baskerville by
Katerprint Co. Ltd, Oxford
Printed in Great Britain at the
University Press, Cambridge

Chapter 1

THERE WAS a way home from school along the beach. It was not a pretty beach, and often the sky was grey, so that you could not see where the sky met the sea. Big rocks of sandstone stuck out into the water. They should have been pink, and you could see that they were if you climbed onto them on a good day, but from the beach they were grey, covered with barnacles.

Where the sea ended the beach was black. It was made of coal.

When they first moved, a month ago, Brian's mother was horrified.

"The children can't go down there," she decided. "They'll be bringing black into the house. Sand I can put up with, but not coal."

Dad was sad. He thought he was doing the right thing, bringing his family to the clean air of the seaside. He had been offered a good job and a house to go with it. They had moved from so far away that none of them had been able to see the town before they actually lived there.

"We'll give it a try, eh?" said Dad, squeezing Brian's hand when Mum went on about the dirt and the inconvenience and the lack of shops.

"You could take them to that nice beach along the way," said Mum.

It was Saturday, and sunny, and Brian was moping round the back door. Brian's little sister gurgled from her playpen, as if she thought it was a nice idea.

Eleanor, the eldest, sniffed.

"I don't want to go to that dirty old place down there," she said.

"Well, we can go to Dunbar every weekend when the weather's fine," said Dad. "There's a bus every half hour."

Brian thought this was not the same at all. If you came to live at the seaside you should be able to go down to your own beach whenever you liked.

But if they could not go to the beach, there were other places. At school Brian found two new friends. Their names were Sandy and Ian.

"Coming to the army camp?" said Sandy after school on the second day.

"What army camp?" said Brian. He knew Mum would say no.

"It's not a real one," said Ian. "Dad says it's left over from the last war. Beach defences. But there are places to go in, and we could play soldiers. Sandy and me do."

"I'm not supposed to go on the beach," said Brian, ashamed.

Sandy looked at him with scorn, but Ian said, "It's not on the beach. Just near it, on the grass. You won't get dirty."

It was nice to have a friend with the same kind of mum, thought Brian.

He was the German, of course, because he was new, and had to be the enemy. Sandy and Ian marched over pretend heather, playing their pretend bagpipes, and shot down his plane from the pill-box. He rolled over the grass in agony. Not in the mud, because he knew that would make Mum cross.

Mum was a little bit cross, because he was late, and because she had not understood the grocer's dialect and bought more sugar than she needed.

However, when Brian came home late at the same time every day she forgot to be angry, and even said, "You're home early," once when Sandy and Ian had gone off to Cubs.

"Why don't you join?" she said. Brian had been wondering whether to ask, in case she said no.

But Brian still wanted to go down to the coal beach to play. One night, when his friends were at Cubs, he went towards the sea, in a hurry, in case he was late back and Mum should be suspicious.

The sea mist was blowing in, and it did not seem far to the edge of the world.

It was mining country. The power station nearby was fed by coal from the pits. Brian wondered whether the black stones on the beach would burn. The tide was up. They would be too wet to burn in any case. He leaned down from the block of stone on which he was standing to feel the gritty sand. It brushed off just like ordinary sand. There was no black dust left on his hands. Mum would not know.

So on the days when Sandy and Ian did not stay behind to play the army game, Brian went down to explore the strange, empty beach.

It was then that the miners went on strike. There'd be no more coal.

Mum patted the fire into shape, heaping the last of the coals towards the back of the fire so that the water would be heated first.

"Why they didn't put immersion heaters into these houses I shall never know," she said.

"We could have one put in," said Dad.

"It's all right for you, out all day," said Mum. "It's far too hot for a fire this weather, but we need water for baths and washing."

"There's coal on the beach," said Brian.

"Don't be silly," said Eleanor in a superior voice. She was doing her homework on the dining-room table. She liked doing homework. Brian thought she was stupid. They did not have homework at his school. "Anyway, you've never been on the beach to know."

"I've heard about the sea-coal on the beach," said Dad. "The coal seam comes right to the surface out in the sea there, and it gets washed ashore like any other kind of rock. I shouldn't think it would be much good for burning, but we could go looking for driftwood."

"It'll be wet as anything," said Mum. "There's not enough heat in this fire to dry anything, and no more coal till goodness knows when."

"We'll have a go anyway," said Dad. "Come on, Brian. Bring that soapbox go-kart of yours. We haven't had it on the road since we came here."

Brian had made it for a race at his old school. It was mostly bits from an old pushchair given to baby Lorraine, but which Mum had scorned as being too scruffy.

"You can't take that old thing outside," said Mum.

"Everybody has one," said Brian.

"Oh, well, if they're all as daft as you."

"You'll get filthy," said Eleanor. She liked to be tidy and clean, just like Mum.

"We'll take off our shoes before we come back inside," said Dad.

The kart was at the back of the cupboard. They had to remove three bicycles, the lawn-mower, all the garden tools and various boxes first.

"My goodness, I wondered where that had gone," said Dad, as a hammer nearly brained him. It fell from a box Brian was lifting over the garden tools.

"We can get at it now," said Brian. "Give us that rake. I'll put it back when you've pulled the kart out."

They wondered whether to dust off the cobwebs, but decided it wasn't worth the bother if driftwood was to be put in it.

"A spot of fog coming up," said Dad as they rattled the kart down the steps to the beach. "I wonder how we're going to get this lot up again."

"We can bring the kart back the long way," said Brian. "There's just one steep bit, and no steps."

"Good man. You know more about this place than I do."

"I come home from school this way." Then he remembered he was not supposed to do this.

"Rather a long way round," said Dad. "How do you get the dirt off so that Mum doesn't notice?"

"It's not dirty," said Brian quickly. "You get bits on your feet, just like sand, but it comes off. I wipe it off on the grass where there's that statue."

"Another time, better ask if you can," said Dad. "Even if you think you're right, better to have things above board."

"You might say no," said Brian.

"True. That's the risk you have to take. Look, we're not the only ones."

Along in the distance there were people with sacks.

"The sacks will be for coal, not firewood, I should think," said Dad.

"Shall we take some and see what happens?"

"Better get both," said Brian.

"Right. You do the wood hunting and I'll do the coal heaving."

They hauled the kart over the jagged rubble of stones and old bricks down to the dark water's edge. Shells gleamed whiter than on ordinary beaches against the black sand.

"My goodness," said Dad, peering at the shells, "a tartan mussel. Can you get anything more Scottish than that?"

Brian came to look, and laughed. It was tartan, black checked over a yellow background.

"Pollution, I suppose. Look at those pipes. We'd better not eat anything from here. Pity, your Mum's good at mussel soup. Ah, a nice lump of coal for our first sackful."

The coal was flat and rounded and very heavy. Dad dropped it into the kart.

"We'd better leave it here, on this

rocky bit, so that the wheels don't get bogged under with the weight. I don't fancy carrying this lot up the beach."

They separated. Brian walked along the shore, listening to the quiet shush of waves as they crept to his feet then ran back. There was not much wood. By the time he had gone halfway to the power station he had found only two soaked splinters and a huge log.

He walked back along the high-tide mark. There was more here. Just as he thought he could carry no more he found an old fish box and loaded all the rest of the wood into it.

"Someone's having trouble," said Dad as he came back to the kart.

"Who?"

"Either the sack boys or that old fellow with a horse and cart. They're having an argument."

They stood and watched for a while. People were waving their arms. They seemed to be angry. Then the cart moved. It was painted green, or had been, along time ago. As it drew nearer Brian saw that the paint was dirty and scratched. The sides were carved in flowing scallops, and its two wheels were banded with iron. The horse had big feet and seemed to have no difficulty walking on the sand.

"Having bother?" said Dad when the old man came within speaking distance.

"It's this strike," said the man. "I've a licence from the council to gather sea-coal here, and the young lads are picking my coal."

Brian felt guilty.

"Do you want ours?" he said.

"Nay, laddie. Yours'll not fill a corner on the cart. But that lot—" he jerked a head at the big boys with their sacks, "they're going to do me out of my job before the week's out. The strike is none of their fault, but I wish they'd not take so much and leave a little for them as has the rights."

Dad was sympathetic, and stood for a while talking to the old man. Brian was bored. He started to tug the kart over the shells and pebbles.

"Coal miners, all of us," said a voice.

He turned and let go the string of his kart to see Sandy grinning at him.

Brian lifted the fish box from the coal in the kart.

"Not much," said Sandy critically. "You'll only get half a fire out of that."

"Two, at least," said Brian, thinking of Mum's fires.

"Wrong sort of coal," said Sandy, looking underneath.

"Why?" said Brian. He saw Dad coming up the beach towards him. "I don't see why we shouldn't try it."

"Don't say I didn't warn you," said Sandy.

Chapter 2

WITH PRIDE, Brian and Dad hauled the kart of coal and wood home. Mum fussed a bit about the dampness of the wood, but said they could dry it out indoors.

"If we go every day we can stack it by the fire, and then it'll be dry enough," said Brian.

"It's getting colder," said Dad, shivering from being outside in the gathering mist. "Soon need the fires on all the time."

"That means no immersion heater, I suppose," said Mum.

"Ordered it already," said Dad cheerfully. "But I don't think you're going to need it. Winter's coming in fast."

"In October!" said Mum.

"You're in Scotland now," said Dad. "Frost in a day or two, I shouldn't wonder."

That night there was a slight frost. Dad rose early and put the fire on for Mum before he went to work.

"I must say your coal is very good," said Mum, bustling in from the sitting room to the kitchen. "The water's getting warm already."

Eleanor and Brian left their breakfasts and went through to look at the sea-coal.

It was burning brightly.

"You win," said Eleanor. "But I bags you always do the coal heaving."

"Cheap, too," said Mum, admiring.

Then the fire spat. It cracked loudly and half a lump sped onto the carpet.

Brian rushed forward to pick it up and yelled at the heat.

"Tongs!" shouted Mum.

There was a smell of burning wool, and another crack, as the carpet was strewn with more hot cinders.

"For heaven's sake," said Eleanor. "Get the fireguard."

Brian suddenly remembered where he had seen it. It was in the back cupboard with the bicycles. He ran through the kitchen to the cupboard. Mum was unstrapping Lorraine from her high chair.

"Can you help me put it up, Mum?" Brian asked, struggling with the pieces. "I'm not quite sure how it goes."

Eleanor swept the bits from the carpet as they fell while Brian and Mum tried to find out how the fireguard fitted together.

"For heaven's sake," said Eleanor, fielding Lorraine for the fourth time, "let's just put the thing against the chimney. Even if it doesn't fit, it'll stop this stuff from sparking out. No, lovely, it's hot!"

They stacked the sections of fire-guard against the chimney and took Lorraine outside.

"Don't think much of your coal," said Eleanor.

"You do the coal heaving next time then," said Brian. "It was Dad anyway. I got the wood."

"That spat too."

"Have you finished your breakfasts?" said Mum. "Time you were off, both of you."

"I'm all coal!" wailed Eleanor. "Thank heavens for a dark uniform. I'll wash my hair tonight." This was to Mum, meaning she needed plenty of water heated.

Ian and Sandy were on their way to school, too.

"What's up?" said Ian when Eleanor had turned down the lane to her school.

"The fire spat all over the floor."

"Told you," said Sandy. "It does if you don't get the right sort. Even then it spits, some of the time."

"Come with us tomorrow night and we'll show you the right bits to pick," said Ian.

"Why not tonight?" said Brian.

"Cub night," said Ian. "Coming?"

Cubs was fun. Brian decided he was going to go in for all the badges. Perhaps he would go in for the Duke of Edinburgh Award when he was old enough. There were enough mountains to practise on, Sandy had said.

He walked home along the beach. There was still a quarter of an hour before Mum expected him home, as Cubs had finished early that night.

It was beginning to get dark. The sky was so clear that he could see the islands in the Firth. All the beach was going grey, sandstone and all. Brian wriggled his shoes in the coal sand. There was a lot of driftwood at the high-tide mark. Someone else was picking it up, but perhaps he could have some. It would keep the fire going, instead of the spitting coal.

It was a very big pile. It looked as though a big wheel was sticking out at the bottom of the pile. Brian realised, suddenly, with a sick feeling in his stomach, what it was.

"You just go for a pint," said a voice, "and people bash up your cart." It was the old man Dad and Brian had met on the beach.

"Where's the horse?" said Brian stupidly, but afraid for it.

"Back in his stable," said the man. "You don't imagine I'd leave him here with those yobbos about? I hadn't collected a full load yet. I was leaving it to the morning." He shook his head. "An old fellow with no pension but what the government gives me."

"Is it just the wheel that's broken?" said Brian.

"It's bad enough about the coal," the man went on bitterly, "but how can I collect any more with one wheel gone?"

Brian was embarrassed. He did not know what to do.

"Can I carry the coal?" he said.

"A wee thing like you? Get off with you. There's not enough muscle in you to carry this load."

"My friends?"

"A few of you, mebbe," said the man. "Perhaps a few of you could manage. It's heavy, mind. Best get your dads."

Brian tore up the beach, and forgot to wipe his shoes on the grass.

"Oh, Brian!" said Mum. "You were told not to go on that beach."

"Where's Dad?" said Brian. "It's that poor old man down on the beach. His cart's been broken, and he wants some help."

Dad was in the next room, watching television.

"Why do you always come when I'm in the middle of a good programme?" he grumbled. "Oh, well, I suppose we'd better go and rescue the old fellow."

"I'll go for Sandy and Ian," said Brian outside, "then I'll meet you down there."

Ian's mother said Ian was almost

ready for bed, and could not go out again. He grinned sheepishly from behind the half open door, until his mother snapped at him to go in by the fire.

But Sandy was up, and outside his front door.

"The old coalman's got a broken wheel," said Brian. "Can you come and help?"

Not only Sandy came, but his father too, a big miner whose arms, Brian felt sure, would get the wheel out of the sand no trouble at all.

"It's all very well getting it out," said Dad, after they had lifted the wreckage from the sand and propped up the cart on a pile of rocks. "What do we do now?"

They all looked at the broken wheel.

"There's not a wheelwright in miles,"

said Sandy's dad. "They're a dying breed."

"Even if I could afford it," said the old man. "With this strike, and they young fellows taking all the sea-coal, I'll not be able to make a living, let alone pay for a new wheel."

"Could we . . . " began Brian.

"I don't see why not," said Sandy. "We'll get enough for ourselves first, but none of that slate stuff you pick up."

"But it's school tomorrow," said Sandy's dad, catching on at once.

"What about school?" said Brian's dad.

"It's the weekend the day after and we can start after school," said Sandy.

"Right, Mr McFadyen," said Sandy's dad in a businesslike way, "the lads will carry your coal for you, till you get the wheel mended."

"You're a good man, though a miner, Mr Watson," said the old man.

"The Black-Sand Miners, that's us," said Sandy.

Chapter 3

IT SEEMED as if the whole school was out on Friday after school, not only girls and boys from Brian's class, but one or two older brothers and sisters as well.

Mr McFadyen was telling Ian the names and addresses of all his customers. Ian wrote everything down, as Mr McFadyen was not so good at writing.

"I went to school," he said, "but only till I was ten. Then I had to help my father on the farm. You don't need book learning for that." Most of Mr McFadyen's customers were old. They had bought the sea-coal for years. It burned with a brighter flame, they said, was hotter and gave less smoke than the coal from the pits.

"What about all that ash?" said Brian. He thought of the grey-white pebbles that were left in the grate at home the morning after their first try at it.

"You don't get so much if you build the fire right," said the lady whose bin they were filling. "Not so much of that big stuff, laddie, or I'll have great lumps left."

Ian obligingly cracked some of the largest lumps with a hammer, left by the bin for that purpose.

"Will you not stop for a scone and jam?" said the customer.

Ian was tempted. Brian could smell the warm steam of baking from her kitchen.

"Come on," said Sandy. "Always thinking of your stomachs. Half of the others will be there and back before we've turned round."

"Sorry, we can't," said Brian.

"Very sorry," said Ian with a longing glance at the kitchen.

They started off, then Brian remembered about the money, and Mr McFadyen saying they were to be sure to collect it and not leave anything on the slate. They had to wait with the delicious smell in their noses while their customer searched for the right coins.

“Right, boys, ninety miles an hour down the hill, and no braking,” shouted Sandy. “Imagine you’re at Musselburgh race course, in for the big prize.”

“I’ll bet horses don’t race on empty stomachs,” grumbled Ian, but turned his kart to the pavement.

"They'll not win on a full one," said Sandy, and pushed off.

It was a marvellous ride. Brian felt the cracks on the stone paving through his behind, doc, doc, doc, all the way to the high street.

Near the bottom of the hill Brian's kart struck a big stone. The wheels went sideways and he reached the kerb rather quickly, before he meant to.

There was no traffic in sight, so instead of putting his heels down, he went on, and bumped through a gap in the houses bordering the beach.

It was one of the gaps with steps. Brian stuck his feet out sideways and fielded his kart down as quickly as he dared. One of the wheels felt loose, but he couldn't stop. He decided to go down to the hard black sand below high-tide mark and meet up with Sandy and Ian that way.

He was so pleased at getting down the steps that the last, big one took him by surprise.

He landed with a bang on bricks and rubble below the sea wall.

"Go away, wee laddie," said a voice.

Brian looked up. A big boy with fair hair cut close to his head was standing over him.

"Before we break your wheels, too," said another voice.

The blond boy said, "Shush!" rather crossly, and Brian saw there were six of them, standing round the battered kart.

"And don't come coaling," said one of them.

Brian's head was aching. But through the hurt he saw the sacks beside the big boys. They must have been the ones who, two days ago, had been arguing with old Mr McFadyen along the beach.

"I don't think I can," said Brian. "It's broken."

"Less of your cheek," said the second boy, smaller, with black, equally short hair.

Brian got up.

"He's got a licence," he said, meaning Mr McFadyen.

"Our dads are miners, and some of us are miners," said the dark boy. He sounded angry. "We're out of work, so should he be."

"You shouldn't have bashed up the old man's wheel, though, Jacko," said the blond boy.

"You're too soft, Charlie," said Jacko. "The way that old boy goes on, he deserved it. Come on, we've got to get the sacks." No one offered to help Brian.

He limped a little, and pulled the kart behind him. Only one wheel had come off, and that seemed to be all right, not even buckled. He could see Sandy and Ian waving at him from along the beach. No one else but Mr McFadyen was there.

He had a stitch, and his head still hurt. The kart was difficult to drag with one wheel in his hand. He sobbed a little when the other front wheel jammed against a rock.

"Come *on*, you thing, get *out*!"

The kart came out, but not the wheel. Brian grabbed the axle with the other wheel, dropped it into the box seat, wondered why he had not done this with the first wheel, dropped that in, then picked up the kart and ran.

He bumped down the beach to Sandy and Ian.

"Sandy . . . " he panted.

"It's a right mess," said Sandy, looking at the damaged kart.

"Those boys. The ones that broke Mr McFadyen's cart . . ."

"Man, you're bleeding," Sandy said, suddenly noticing.

"It's them that broke the wheel, they said so," said Brian. "I'm all right. Really."

"Did they touch you?" said Sandy darkly.

"No, but it was them."

Brian turned to his kart and tried to fit the axle back on.

"It's split, laddie," said Mr McFadyen. "You'll be needing a wheelwright, the same as meself."

"We'll get them," said Sandy fiercely.

"It wasn't their fault. I fell down the wall," said Brian, anxious to be fair.

"Not their fault, bashing up my cart!" shouted Mr McFadyen.

"That's it, then," said Sandy. "It's war. The Black-Sand Miners against Them!"

But it was not until the next morning, which was Saturday, that the Black-Sand Miners had a chance to discuss what was to be done with the wheel wreckers.

"There's six of them, and they're big," said Ian.

"And we've still to get the coal," said Sandy, "so whatever we do it had better be quick."

"Get them to help with the picking," said Brian, not very seriously.

They sat on the sea wall, thinking.

"I've got it," said Sandy. "What do they do with these sackfuls they collect?"

"I've seen them loading up an old van," said Ian. "One of them drives the van, and the rest of them have got motorbikes."

"And how many of us are there?"

"Fifteen or sixteen? I don't really know." Ian began to count.

"Don't bother," said Sandy. "There are more than you can count quickly. Right, most of us will be here, collecting for Mr McFadyen – and while they're doing that, us three will be letting the air out of their bike tyres."

Brian was shocked. “You can’t do that.”

“Why not? They did break Mr McFadyen’s wheel. We’re just going to let theirs down.”

Everybody but Sandy, Ian and Brian were to go on collecting coal in their karts, just as they had the evening before. While the big boys were on the beach with their sacks Sandy, who for some reason knew how to let air out of tyres with a matchstick, would be playing football with his friends on the green by the High Street shops.

There was plenty of time to eat before the plan. Sandy had been given money for fish and chips from the shop, and he brought them, golden and savoury in their white paper, to the beach. Ian had been made to sit down to mince and cabbage and potatoes, but accepted two chips all the same. Brian had made his own sandwiches.

There was a loud clatter of motorbikes from the High Street.

"This is it," said Sandy. "Motorbikes. I know their noise."

The Black-Sand Miners were beginning to arrive with their karts. Brian wished he could have brought his, but it was still outside the house, its two back wheels lying against the wall.

"You've been seen?" said Ian when he came back.

"No," said Brian. "I was careful. But I know which van and bikes they are."

"So do I," said Sandy. "Right, gang?"

The rest of the class spread out along the beach and began to gather coal.

"Right," said Sandy suddenly, in Brian's ear.

The ball, white with black lozenges, sped past Brian's nose.

Brian raced after it and kicked it up the beach. He was proud of that kick, and stood admiring it until Sandy's yell made him run over the rubble to the sea wall.

It was a beautiful kick. Brian and Ian both tore after it. Ian bounced it up the steps, pretending he was goalie. Sandy argued fiercely that he should have headed it, but all the time the ball was travelling in the direction of the cars.

"Now," said Sandy.

Brian and Ian dribbled round the motorbikes. Sandy lay on the ground, pretending to field the ball. Two policemen walked past, their chequered flat caps so different from the high helmets Brian knew from the south. They smiled at the boy's game, and one of them kicked the ball across to the motorbikes.

"That will do," said Sandy quietly, and pulled out his matchstick. Ian and Brian kicked the ball round the bikes. It seemed like years before Sandy had finished.

"Right," said Sandy, "That should teach them."

Brian felt guilty, until he thought of the old man's cart-wheel, and felt better.

They kicked the ball back to the beach and helped the coal heavers.

Brian had filled Sandy's kart and went off after what looked like a good lot of coal, away from the others. He bent to pick up a large piece and looked up to find the six boys beside him.

"It was you," said the one called Jacko.

"Me?" said Brian. His heart was thumping. "I'm helping the others. My kart won't go."

"Nor will my motorbike. I saw you playing football."

Brian looked round. His friends were a very long way away.

Jacko grabbed him by the arm and led him up the beach back to the cars. The other big boys followed behind. Brian looked round desperately, but the Black-Sand Miners were too busy, their eyes on the ground, looking for coal.

"Sandy! Ian!" screamed Brian.

The wind blew a scurry of old sweet papers past his feet. He could hear the high voices of his friends, but his own voice was ripped away in the other direction, to join the pale smoke of the power station.

Jacko gave his arm a mean twist.

"Don't hurt him, Jacko," said the blond boy. "He'll pump them up all right."

"He'd better," growled Jacko.

It was a foot pump, a red thing on a heavy spring. Charlie fitted the end of it onto the valve, just like an ordinary bicycle pump.

"You step on it," he said. "Push your foot up and down like this."

"Don't do it all for him," said Jacko.

It was impossible. Brian's leg muscles were too weak to push the spring down. He tried jumping on it, which was a little better.

Sandy and Ian peeped from the side of one of the shops. Brian saw them out of the corner of his eye. So did one of the six big boys. There was a sudden scuffle, and his friends were beside him.

"Well, it was a good try," said Sandy. "If we both shove with our hands we might do it."

It took a long time, but at last the blond boy said it would do.

"Now you stop pinching the coal," threatened Jacko, "and leave the bikes alone, right?"

"Round two to them," said Sandy

crossly as they went back to the beach.

"But we're not pinching their coal," pointed out Brian. "It's really Mr McFadyen's coal – we're only helping him."

"That's true," said Sandy, brightening. "Right, we'll get everyone we can to help, and if the old man goes to his customers and asks them not to buy the sea-coal from that lot then we've won the next round — and with the law on our side, too!"

Chapter 4

"STORM COMING UP," said Dad on Sunday morning.

Brian had got up early, by arrangement with Sandy and Ian, to start work while the tide was at its lowest. But when he got downstairs he found his watch was wrong, and there was another hour before he need go and knock on Sandy's door. To fill in time, he made a pot of tea and took some up to his parents in bed. He had never seen the view from their window before, and had not realised you could see the sea from it.

"It looks clear," he said. "The islands look as if they're floating on air."

"That means bad weather," said Dad.

"Good thing there's no school," said Mum sleepily.

"Better go and collect as much coal as we can before it starts raining," said Brian. "I'll have breakfast when I come back."

He met Sandy on the way to his house.

"My dad says there's a storm coming up," said Sandy.

"So does mine," said Brian.

The shore was deserted, apart from a black mongrel, busy with his own scavenging on the high-tide line.

"We're not going to get much today," puffed Sandy. "Help me with this lump, it's about a sackful in itself. And look – Dad was right."

Brian looked. The sky was very dark and on each of the waves which had built up without them noticing was a white topping like the squiggly cream you get on shop cakes.

"Tide's coming in fast too," he said.

Suddenly the beach seemed full of people. Ian ran down to join Sandy and Brian. Then the great noise of a motor-bike engine started up, and the cold salt smell of the beach was overpowered by hot exhaust fumes.

"He's mad," said Ian.

Jacko and his motorbike had bumped down the sea wall, turned in a shower of dark sand, and roared up the beach towards the power station.

"He'll get grit in his engine," said Brian.

"Oh, leave him alone," said Sandy impatiently. "We want to pick this stuff before the storm really hits us."

It was not easy. Jacko rode the motorbike at great speed along the hard sand below the tide line, drove up to the knot of children, and, as they scattered in fear, turned so that the tyres threw up great screens of grit into their faces and over the karts.

"Show off!" yelled Ian when he had been sprayed for the second time.

"Silly fool!" shouted Sandy after tipping the grains from his kart for the third time.

Then Jacko, who seemed annoyed that he was only irritating them and not really frightening them, began really to show off.

He roared the bike up the steps, balancing with his legs as the machine bumped and rattled and skidded, heaving the front wheel up to each next step. Then, as he had done the first time they saw him, he did a spectacular jump off the sea wall to land in another biting spray of sharp sand.

The bike groaned and roared and spat. Jacko let in the clutch again and sped, it seemed very fast, towards the edge of the sea. The bike kissed the edge of the waves, swept away, went back, and finally leaped off towards the power station, all the time no more than an inch from the edge of the water.

He turned away to the power station, and the Black-Sand Miners stood in a little crowd, watching as the machine grew smaller and smaller, its noise no more than that of a gnat.

"He's coming back," said Brian.

The gnat sound grew to a mosquito, then to a bumble bee, then suddenly, with the shattering sound of a chain-saw, it was almost upon them. The crowd jumped, some to one side, some to another, and Jacko did a double swerve. Grit splashed over them, in their eyes, and Jacko roared on, looking and laughing.

Then something happened. The bike seemed to go out of control. It skidded again, and then, as it reached the edge of the waves, it slid. The bike fell, Jacko fell, and there was a tangle of boy and machine on the black sand.

"He's stuck," said Brian.

"You might help!" yelled Jacko. His voice was squawky, not deep and threatening as before. His foot had caught in the front fork of the bike as it went over.

The Black-Sand Miners went over to look.

"We could try pulling his boot off," suggested Ian after they had tugged at Jacko to no effect.

Jacko could not reach down to unlace it, so Brian did. However his foot was caught so fast that even that did not help.

Then Sandy suddenly turned and beckoned the others away. They looked startled, but followed him.

"We could get Mr McFadyen's horse to pull the bike up," he said when out of earshot.

Brian looked back. The sky was as grey as pencil lead, and as heavy as a lumpy pillow. The whipped cream on top of the waves was piling high. A squirt of it lapped the front wheel of Jacko's bicycle and he shouted at them in terror.

"Where are you going? Help me!"

"Don't say anything," ordered Sandy.

"He's really frightened," said Brian, obeying.

"Let him be frightened," said Sandy, and clambered up the steps.

But to Brian's relief, as they got to the top, there was Mr McFadyen and his horse.

"You're early," said the old man.

"Mr McFadyen," said Sandy imperiously. One of the big boys has got stuck in the sand . . ."

"Showing off," said Ian.

"And we can't get him out – he's too heavy," explained Brian.

"We really ought to leave him there," said Ian, "but I suppose it would be mean."

"Tide's coming in, you see," said Sandy.

"And a storm's coming up," said Brian.

Mr McFadyen, with great deliberation, led the horse down the steps, with many cries of encouragement. If Brian had not been so worried he would have noticed that the horse put its great feet securely on each uneven step, as if he had been doing it for years, which indeed he had. But at last, the animal was safely on the rubble below the sea wall, and paced steadily across the sand towards Jacko.

“I’m stuck,” said Jacko when they reached him, his eyes not dark with annoyance any more but wide with his fear.

"Aye, I ken that," said Mr McFadyen, not at all concerned, though the water had crept, alarmingly swiftly, right over the front wheel and over the trapped boot. "Just don't bother yourself. Boys, there's a rope the fish man has in his back shop."

With infinite patience, and a lot of groans from Jacko, he edged the foot out of the boot until the big boy was free.

"Get out, then," commanded Mr McFadyen.

"I – I mean, it hurts."

"Stay there and drown, then," said the old man cheerfully, and watched while Jacko crawled away from the waves with a little return of his old ill-nature.

And then Sandy and Ian raced down the beach with the rope. Nobody said anything, but Mr McFadyen looped the rope round the bike and harnessed the other end by a succession of loops and knots to the horse. Then the old man slapped his horse on the flank. The animal walked forward, and the rope tightened. His hooves slipped in the sand, and went on slipping.

"A wee tug from the ranks," called out Mr McFadyen.

Everyone went willingly to the taut rope, and tugged.

Slowly the motorbike slurped in the wet sand, made a little whirlpool in the rising tide, and with a burp worthy of Sandy's dad, slid out of its bed and rolled up above the edge of the sea.

Jacko struggled up the beach on his behind, backwards, till he was level with the old man.

"Mr McFadyen," he said, as if he didn't want to be heard at all.

"Aye?"

"My father's a wheelwright," he said. "I mean, my father was a wheelwright before there wasn't enough work in the trade and he went down the pits with my uncles. He'll mend your wheel for you."

Sandy, Brian and Ian stopped hauling, though the bike was not yet out of danger.

"Go on, laddies," said Mr McFadyen. "Keep tugging. Is that so?" he said to Jacko. "That would be a kind thought. But you'd better put the thought in to his mind before you make any rash promises."

"No, really, he will. Charlie, that's my friend, he went and told somebody, and it got round to my dad. He was fair angry. He said he'd mend it, and I've to pay for anything he needs to do it." Then he added ashamed, "He said if I'd got a trade like yours I wouldn't behave so daft."

"He's probably right," said Mr McFadyen cheerfully. "But it's very kind of him to offer, and I'll be glad to have the wheel mended. The wee ones have been a great help, but they'll be back at the school tomorrow and I'm too old to carry sacks. I'm too old to carry you either, lad, so you'd better crawl up before the tide gets you."

Jacko shivered suddenly and the water caught up with his foot.

"Want a pull?" said Brian, and he put his hands under Jacko's armpits.

"Come on, wee one," said someone else, and pulled him out of the way with strong arms. It was Jacko's friend, Charlie. "What have you done, Jacko, bust it?"

The other big boys had unhitched the horse from Jacko's bike and righted it. They all, the old man, big boys and children, stood around awkwardly. Then the first heavy drops of rain began to fall.

"Better take him to the hospital," called Mr McFadyen, "just to make sure."

Everyone had started to run. A

splash of rain hit Brian on the back of his neck and ran down inside his jersey.

"Come to our house!" yelled Sandy. His kart rattled behind him, sea-coal jumping out back onto the beach.

"I'll go home first!" Brian shouted.

"You're wet," said Dad when Brian slammed through the back door, quite out of breath. There was a glorious smell of bacon in the kitchen.

"It's your storm," said Brian.

"Go in and sit by the fire," said Mum. "I'll put an egg in the pan for you. Get me any coal this morning?"

"Sandy's got some. I'm going round there after."

And he went into the sitting room where the sea-coal fire spat and crackled warmly in the grate.